Tillie
and
the Wall

Leo Lionni

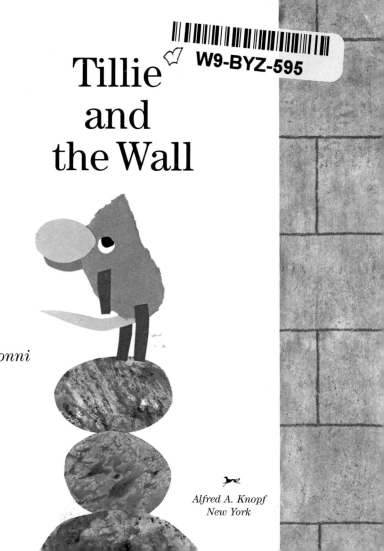

Alfred A. Knopf
New York

The wall had been there ever since the mice could remember. They never paid attention to it. They never asked themselves what was on the other side, nor, for that matter, if there were another side at all. They went about their business as if the wall didn't exist.

The mice loved to talk. They chatted endlessly about this and that, but no one ever mentioned the wall. Only Tillie, the youngest, would stare at it, wondering about the other side.

At night, while the others were asleep, she would lie in her bed of straw, wide awake, imagining beyond the wall a beautiful, fantastic world inhabited by strange animals and plants.

"We *must* see the other side," she told her friends. "Let us try to climb." They tried, but as they climbed, the wall seemed higher and higher.

With a long, rusty nail they tried to make a hole to peep through. "It is only a question of patience!" said Tillie. But after working an entire morning they gave up, exhausted, without having made even a dent in the hard stone.

"The wall must end *somewhere*," Tillie said. They walked and walked for many hours. The wall apparently had no end.

But one day, not far from the wall, Tillie saw a worm digging itself into the black earth. How could she not have thought of that before? Why hadn't anyone thought of that before?

Full of excitement, Tillie began to dig.
She dug and she dug . . .

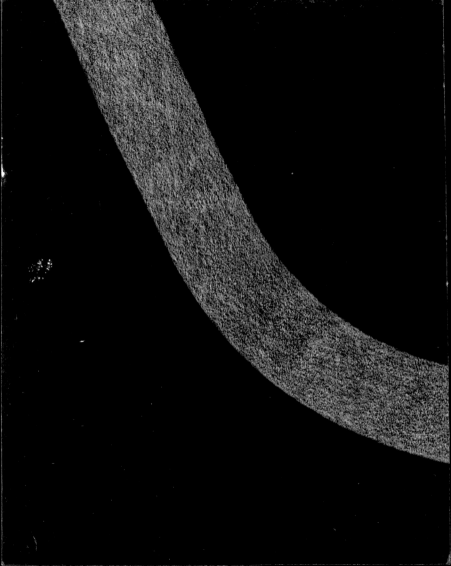

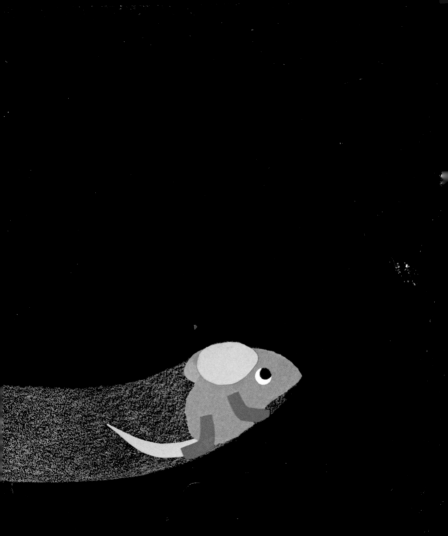

until suddenly, almost blinded by the bright sunlight, she was on the other side of the wall! She couldn't believe her eyes: before her were mice, regular mice.

The mice gave Tillie a great welcome party.
They took her to their celebration pebble
(had she seen that before somewhere?).
They made speeches in her honor and
waved flags.

Then they decided to go through
Tillie's tunnel to see for themselves
what the other side was like. One by
one they followed Tillie.

And when the mice on Tillie's side of the wall saw what Tillie had discovered, there was another party. The mice threw confetti. Everyone shouted "TIL-LIE, TIL-LIE, TIL-LIE!" and they carried Tillie high in the air in triumph.

Since that day the mice go freely from one side of the wall to the other, and they always remember that it was Tillie who first showed them the way.